Leonardo DiCaprio

After first appearing on TV in commercials for Matchbox cars, Leonardo got his first real break by playing a homeless kid on the hit sitcom *Growing Pains* opposite Kirk Cameron.

By his nineteenth birthday, he had earned Golden Globe and Academy Award nominations as best supporting actor for *What's Eating Gilbert Grape,* recognitions for which most actors strive their entire careers.

At the helm of the most expensive motion picture of all time, *Titanic,* Leo proved his worth as a thrilling and romantic lead actor. With several major upcoming films, Leonardo won't be releasing his hold on the box office anytime soon. This heartthrob is here to stay!

What is he really like? What are his future plans? Could *you* be the girl for him?

Read all about *your* favorite leading man:

Leonardo DiCaprio.

Biographies from Archway Paperbacks

Hanson: MMMBop to the Top by Jill Matthews
Jonathan Taylor Thomas: Totally JTT! by Michael-Anne Johns
Prince William: The Boy Who Will Be King by Randi Reisfeld
Taylor Hanson: Totally Taylor! by Nancy Krulik
Isaac Hanson: Totally Ike! by Nancy Krulik
Zac Hanson: Totally Zac! by Matt Netter
The Ultimate Hanson Trivia Book by Matt Netter
Leonardo DiCaprio: A Biography by Nancy Krulik
Will Power!: A Biography of Will Smith by Jan Berenson

SPORTS

Grant Hill: A Biography
Michael Jordan: A Biography
Shaquille O'Neal: A Biography
Tiger Woods: A Biography
Ken Griffey, Jr.: A Biography
  by Bill Gutman
Skating for the Gold: Michelle Kwan & Tara Lipinski
  by Chip Lovitt

INSPIRATIONAL

Warriors Don't Cry: A Searing Memoir of the Battle to Integrate
  Little Rock's Central High by Melba Pattillo Beals
To the Stars: The Autobiography of George Takei, Star Trek's Mr.
  Sulu by George Takei

LEONARDO DiCAPRIO:
A BIOGRAPHY

NANCY KRULIK

AN ARCHWAY PAPERBACK
Published by POCKET BOOKS
New York London Toronto Sydney Tokyo Singapore

AN ARCHWAY PAPERBACK *Original*

An Archway Paperback published by
POCKET BOOKS, a division of Simon & Schuster Inc.
1230 Avenue of the Americas, New York, NY 10020

ISBN: 0-671-02486-8

First Archway Paperback printing April 1998

10 9 8

AN ARCHWAY PAPERBACK and colophon are registered trademarks of Simon & Schuster Inc.

Back cover photo courtesy of Photofest

Printed in the U.S.A.

IL 5+

For Danny B.

CONTENTS

LEONARDO DiCAPRIO:
A BIOGRAPHY

1

RISING STAR IN THE
LAND OF THE RISING SUN

"Leo! Leo! Leo!"

The crowd of screaming fans outside Tokyo's Orchard Hall Theater was already six rows deep by the time the limousines pulled up. It was November 1, 1997, and the new movie, *Titanic,* was making its world premiere at the Tokyo International Film Festival.

Titanic may have been the headlining film at the festival, but it was the movie's star, Leonardo DiCaprio, that was making headlines. From the moment it was announced that Leo would attend the premiere, fans had become fanatical about finding a good viewing spot outside the theater. In fact, Leo-mania had become so strong in Japan that Twentieth Century Fox (*Titanic*'s international distributor) provided the twenty-three-year-old star with forty-nine security guards. That was a good move. As soon as Leo's limo turned the corner, the fans made a mad dash for the car, knocking over many of the guards and policemen, hoping to get a glimpse of Leo's bright blue-green eyes, blond hair, and shy smile.

A glimpse was about all the fans would get before the Fox guards quickly hustled Leo past the crowds and into the theater, where he was again greeted by screaming fans. When Leo took the stage just before the film began, he declared that his Japanese fans were among the "Best and most loyal in the world." This, of course, made the crowd go wild. Leo didn't have to say another word, which was a good thing, since he's petrified of speaking in public.

It's official. Leonardo DiCaprio is now a worldwide superstar, a member of Hollywood's elite, or, as Leo would have said in his youth, part of that *other* Hollywood. Leo has lived all of his life in tinsel town. But the Hollywood Leo knew as a boy was far from shimmering. . . .

2

IN THE BEGINNING

Leonardo Wilhelm DiCaprio was born on November 11, 1974. Before his birth, Leo's mother, Irmelin, already knew he was a take-charge kind of kid. He even had a hand (or was that a foot?) in choosing his own name. While Irmelin was pregnant she received a strong kick from her baby at the very moment she was looking at a Leonardo da Vinci painting in a museum in Italy. Irmelin took that as a sign and decided to name her son Leonardo. (Good thing Leo was a boy, huh?)

Irmelin had met Leo's father, George Di-Caprio, in college. The two married and moved to Los Angeles, eager to settle down and raise a family, despite the fact that they had very little money. Unfortunately, the stress of trying to be parents with a low cash flow became too much for the DiCaprios. They separated before Leo turned one.

Still, Irmelin and George were determined to work as a team to raise their only child. Although Leo lived with his mom, he spent a great deal of time at his father's house. Leo knows how lucky he is to be close to both parents. After all, not all kids who come from divorced families have that opportunity.

"I've never missed out on a so-called normal father-son relationship, because my dad was always there for me," Leo says gratefully.

Irmelin and George were not your typical parents. They were extremely liberal ex-hippie types, with a group of exotic friends. Some of Leo's earliest memories are of sitting down to dinner with guests such as comic-book artist Robert Crumb and rebel novelist Hubert Selby, Jr.

Leo asserts that his childhood was not some sort of bizarre early-seventies commune experience, though. "We're not the hippie family who only eats organic and the children meditate," he says, "but we're not apple pie and Republican, either."

That's for sure. Having really cool parents allows a kid the freedom to express himself, but Leo acknowledges that having such unusual parents does have its drawbacks—he had nothing to rebel against. "Whatever I did would be something they'd already done. I mean, my dad would welcome it if I got a nose ring!" he laughs.

When Leonardo was a kid, his father created and distributed underground comic books from his garage. His mother worked at several odd jobs, including one as a legal secretary. There was never much money around when Leo was growing up. In fact for a time, Leo and his mom lived in a very rough area of Hollywood, surrounded by prostitutes and drug addicts.

"I lived in the ghettos of Hollywood," Leo says. "My mom thought Hollywood was the place where all the great stuff was going on. But meanwhile it was a disgusting place to be."

Still, Leo remembers his childhood happily, mostly because his parents were around for him a lot. While they couldn't afford to take their son on fancy excursions, they always found inexpensive ways to have fun. They visited art museums, took Leo on pony rides, and encouraged him to express his creative side.

At age five, Leo had his first acting experience. It was a disaster.

Leo was scheduled to be one of the children on *Romper Room,* a preschool television show that took place on a schoolroom set. Leo has always said that school wasn't his thing. Apparently make-believe school wasn't Leo's thing either. He was fired from the show on his very first day of work for disruptive behavior. It would be nine years before Leo went in front of the cameras again.

3

BITTEN BY THE BUG

By the time he was fourteen, Leo was getting a little tired of living life on the poor side of the Hollywood tracks. It wasn't that he was obsessed with money for himself, it was more that he felt his mother deserved something better. (That's a theme in Leo's life. Now that he's got some cash, he's building a vacation house for his mom.)

The first person Leo knew who made a lot of money was his father's stepson, Adam Starr. (Adam is the son of George DiCaprio's second wife.) Adam and Leo were close, although not as close as real brothers who live in the same house might be. Still Leo looked up to Adam, so when he heard that Adam had been cast in a Golden Grahams cereal commercial, he was very impressed. When he discovered that Adam had made thousands of dollars in fees and residuals from the commercial, Leo was more than impressed, he was thrilled. Leo figured he'd finally found his way out of the Hollywood ghetto. (Even though most of the money earned by child actors is put in a trust until they are adults, the children and their parents are allowed to spend some of their earnings—and that alone would be enough to get Leo and his mom to a better place.)

Once Leo expressed an interest in performing, his ever-supportive parents took him to interview after interview with talent agents. But Leo's quick fix for poverty turned out to be anything but quick. For starters, finding an agent proved to be a difficult task. One agent didn't like his hair. Another agent didn't like his name (he suggested he change it to Lenny Williams). Finally Leo signed up with an agency where a family friend worked.

When it came to getting roles, Leo had a lot in his favor. He was really adorable, even back then, and he has always looked young for his age. When you're a child actor, that comes in very handy. A fourteen-year-old who looks ten can memorize parts quicker and take direction better than an actual ten-year-old can, so he's more likely to get cast. That may explain why the first commercial teenage Leo did was for toys. He played a ten-year-old boy who loved Matchbox cars.

After the Matchbox cars ad, commercial jobs came pouring in. So did the cash. But while the money did make things easier for Leo, acting in TV commercials just didn't satisfy his creative urges. He wanted the chance to develop a character for longer than thirty or sixty seconds.

Leo got his chance to work outside commercials in two educational films called *Mickey's Safety Club*, and *How to Deal with a Parent Who Takes Drugs*. It was while he was doing these educational films that Leo was given two TV guest-starring roles that would define the troubled-teen persona that would follow him for several years. He appeared as a boy gone wrong in an episode of *The New Adventures of Lassie* and in a similar role on an episode of the TV version of *The Outsiders*. Those two roles gave Leo a chance to show just what kind of dramatic actor he was capable of becoming. The parts were still only one-time deals, however. Leo was looking for something that would last a little longer, a role that he could develop over a number of weeks. His very next job was a dream come true.

Leo was cast as a teenage alcoholic on the

daytime drama (that's TV talk for soap opera), *Santa Barbara*. As a soap-opera actor, Leo was given the opportunity to play the same character every day. He learned to work with the writers to help the character develop just as a real person would in a similar situation.

Working on *Santa Barbara* may have been good for Leo's acting chops, but it didn't do much for his schoolwork. He was only fifteen at the time, and by law Leo could only work half a day on the show. The other half of his work day was split between doing his schoolwork with an on-set tutor and working with one of his parents on memorizing his lines for the next day. Usually, the lines took precedence in Leo's mind.

Leo did not become a regular on *Santa Barbara*—the role was always intended to be limited to a few months—but just as that job ended, opportunity knocked on Leo's door once again. This time he was cast as Garry Buckman on a new half-hour sitcom called *Parenthood*. TV's *Parenthood* was based on the successful movie of the same name, so Leo and the show's producers had big hopes for a long run.

No such luck. While audiences flocked to see the film, which starred Steve Martin and was directed by Ron Howard, very few people tuned in to see the weekly TV show, which had a less well-known cast. *Parenthood* was canceled after just four months on the air.

Four months was long enough, though, for teenage girls to get a good look at Leo's sizzling smile and bright blue-green eyes. Suddenly Leo found himself on the covers of teen magazines, being touted as what he not-so-fondly calls, "The hunk of the month."

If Leo's fans were disappointed that their hot new hunk had been yanked off the air so quickly, their emotions were quickly lifted, just as soon as it was announced that the hit series *Growing Pains* was about to add a new character —a homeless boy named Luke Bower, played by Leonardo DiCaprio.

4

LEO'S GROWING PAINS

Playing Luke Bower on *Growing Pains* was a big break for Leonardo. He was on a show that was already a success, ensuring that a large audience would see his work. The show, which was about a psychologist (played by Alan Thicke), his reporter wife (played by Joanna Kerns), and their three children (Kirk Cameron, Tracey Gold, and Jeremy Miller), had been a huge hit for six years. Leo was joining a cast of top-notch professionals.

A great deal of *Growing Pains'* success had to be credited to the teen-idol status of the series star, Kirk Cameron. Kirk had already appeared on the covers of more fan magazines than he could count. But he was getting older, and the producers needed to find a way to keep that fan base from leaving the show. Their solution was to bring in Leo's character, a homeless boy who had come to live with the Seavers.

Leonardo learned a lot from his work on *Growing Pains.* He discovered that he was brave enough to cry on camera, even though he was embarrassed the first time he had to do it in front of a studio audience. (Leo says that his trick to crying on cue is to think of his mother in pain. That unbearable thought can get him to sob in an instant.) He also worked on his comic timing, a skill many actors believe to be far more difficult than acting in a straight dramatic role.

Almost as important as his acting lessons were the life lessons he learned from Kirk Cameron. Kirk had already gone through the shock of suddenly becoming a teen idol and he was always there to lend an ear or give advice when the pressures of stardom got to Leo.

"He gave me a constant, positive perspective on life," Leo says of his discussions with Kirk Cameron.

"We had long talks about [teen idol stardom]," Kirk Cameron says today. "I told him to have fun with it. I was always grateful to the fans, and so is he."

Growing Pains would run for one final season after Leo joined the cast. Ironically, Leo wasn't in the last four episodes of the show. He'd already left to take a lead role in a movie. The film was accurately entitled, *This Boy's Life.*

Leo was just sixteen when he was cast in the film. He calls his experience on *This Boy's Life* educational and exciting.

"There was a big cattle call, with thousands of young actors from all over the world auditioning for the part," he says of his tryout for the role of Tobias Wolff. "I think it was probably my ignorance—not being afraid of (Robert) De Niro at the time—that got me the part.

"It was a huge role for a kid that age to get, and I got the opportunity to work with Robert De Niro right from the start. It was a complete learning experience for me, watching De Niro acting every day. Like a drama school. That showed me what real acting is all about and it molded me for the rest of my career."

While Tracey Gold and Leo were working together on *Growing Pains,* she told a reporter that Leo was "a great actor who would do great movies." Tracey's prediction came true. After the rave reviews Leo got for his role in *This Boy's Life,* one thing was crystal clear. The future of Leo's career was not to be found on television. It was to be found in the movies.

5

MAKING IT IN THE MOVIES

A mentally challenged eighteen-year-old climbing fanatic. A high school basketball star who turns to drugs for comfort. A young poet struggling with his sexuality. An angry young man just sprung from a stint in a mental institution. A rebellious teen who risks all for the woman he loves. A fun-loving, smart-alecky artist who wins the heart of a wealthy young woman.

It's hard to believe that one young actor could make all of those characters come alive. But over the past ten years, Leonardo has managed to create characters that are as different as they are believable. Of all the actors in his generation, Leo is rapidly being acknowledged as one of the few capable of displaying a range of human emotions on a grand scale.

The key to Leo's success is that he is more concerned with playing the character on the screen than he is with looking good for the camera. Leo doesn't want to be appreciated for his looks; he wants to be respected for his acting. That's why he had no problem altering his gorgeous smile with a set of false teeth to play Arnie Grape in *What's Eating Gilbert Grape.* It's also why he chose to be in *The Basketball Diaries,* allowing the makeup crew to turn him into a gaunt, filthy, homeless heroin addict, even though playing a pretty-boy comedy role would have skyrocketed his career to the top far faster.

In fact, throughout his career, there was only one thing Leo wasn't willing to do for a character: there was no way he was putting on tights to play Romeo. He says he was afraid of being called "a fuffy." You read right, a fuffy. Only Leo knows for sure what he meant by that, but he has said that by getting rid of Romeo's tights, he feels he got rid of some of the misconceptions about the character.

"Baz [*Romeo and Juliet* director Baz Luhrmann] wanted to understand it and get rid of the stereotypes," he says of *Romeo and Juliet.* "Like the belief that Romeo is dopey and lovey-dovey and that it's a corny story." Once again Leo's instincts worked best. His portrayal of Romeo brought classic Shakespearean drama to a new height.

The best way to understand Leonardo DiCaprio the actor is to study his movies. And the best place to do that is right here. So get out your tickets. We're going to the movies.

CRITTERS 3: Leo has made many movies that he is extremely proud of. Unfortunately *Critters 3* isn't one of them. This third installment in the *Critters* horror movie series was made just after Leo finished his *Parenthood* stint. It features Leo as the son of a frightening slum lord. In the movie, a single father brings a few Critters into an old tenement building by mistake (they hide out in his camper). As in the first two *Critters* movies, the strange, starving Critters are searching for another helping of human flesh. It's up to Leo to hold the creatures at bay until help can arrive.

Critters 3 was such a bad movie, many people are trying to forget about it. Often, when biographies of Leo appear in magazines, they begin his filmography with *This Boy's Life,* but don't you believe it. *Critters 3* was Leo's big screen debut. (Hey, everyone's entitled to *one* mistake, right?)—*(This film is rated PG-13)*

POISON IVY: Keep your eyes glued to the screen when you watch this flick, which marked a big comeback for Drew Barrymore. If you blink, you may miss Leo in his short cameo role as Guy #1 (his role was so small, it didn't even rate a name). Even though Leo doesn't have much screen time, his fans will probably catch this movie in which a girl named Ivy (played by Drew Barrymore) moves in with her newly married aunt. The aunt's new family includes a reclusive fellow teen, Sylvie (played by *Roseanne*'s Sara Gilbert). Sylvie is at first fascinated and later repulsed by Ivy, when the wild girl makes a pass at Sylvie's dad.—*(This film is rated R)*

THIS BOY'S LIFE: Imagine what it would be like to live in an isolated area with a stepfather who is mentally and physically capable of killing you. That's what Leo had to do in order to play the role of Tobias Wolff in *This Boy's Life*. Like many of the films Leo has taken on in his career, *This Boy's Life* is a true story. It vividly describes the horrors author Tobias Wolff had to endure while growing up in Washington state with his mother, stepfather, and step siblings.

Robert De Niro plays Dwight, Tobias's stepfather. In the hands of this master actor,

Dwight is a truly terrifying creature. He is both treacherous and vain, as well as conniving and cruel. He believes in control through physical and verbal domination.

It would take an amazing actor to steal a movie from Robert De Niro. Leo is just that kind of actor. When the movie was released, movie critic Lon Ponschock declared that "Leonardo DiCaprio as young Tobias is the real star of the picture." And reviewer James Berardinelli said that "Leonardo DiCaprio . . . shows unexpected passion and raw ability in his role as Tobias." *People* magazine added to the rave reviews, stating that "Leonardo DiCaprio, in his first major movie role, carried the film with impressive ease, letting you see the hurt beneath this kid's affected toughness."—*(This film is rated R)*

WHAT'S EATING GILBERT GRAPE: Poor Gilbert Grape. His life in Endora, Iowa just isn't what it should be. He's stuck in a dead end job bagging groceries, his overweight mother hasn't left the house in seven years, and his sisters are always fighting. To top it all off, he's left having to take care of his seventeen-year-old mentally challenged brother, who has a habit of climbing to the top of the town water tower, much to the dismay of the local police. Gilbert's life takes an amazing turn, though, when he meets a fun-loving, worldly girl named Becky (Juliette Lewis), who shows Gilbert what fun life can really be.

What's Eating Gilbert Grape was meant to be a showcase for Johnny Depp. After all, it was Johnny who had the title role in the movie. And it was Johnny who got the girl. But it was Leo's portrayal of Arnie Grape, Gilbert's brain-damaged brother, that had the critics raving.

"DiCaprio's characterization of Arnie is a startling tour de force, a marvelous, completely unself-conscious performance," Hal Hinson of the *Washington Post* wrote in his review of the film.

Leo received nominations in the best supporting actor category for both the Golden Globe and Academy Awards. And even though Leo's name wasn't in the envelope at either awards ceremony, his portrayal of Arnie Grape cemented his place in Hollywood history.

By the way, please don't feel too bad that Leo didn't go home with that Oscar. He says he's glad he didn't win. If he had, he would have had to go on stage and make a speech, and the thought of speaking in front of millions of viewers scares him to death.

"I worried that I would slip up or do something horrible," Leo says of his thoughts during the Academy Awards show. "I was shaking in my seat with this fixed smile on my face."

In the end, the best supporting actor honor went to Tommy Lee Jones for his role in *The Fugitive.* Nobody in that audience was happier for Tommy—or more relieved—than sweet, shy Leo!—*(This film is rated PG-13)*

TOTAL ECLIPSE: Making *Total Eclipse* was a huge gamble for Leo. He played Arthur Rimbaud, a young poet involved with Paul Verlaine, a glum older man. Kissing another man on film was a daring move for Leo, and one that didn't pay off—at least not at the box office. Leo's fan base wasn't as strong then as it is today, and they didn't follow him to the theaters. Still, Leo vows he'd make the movie again.

"I like the film for what it is," Leo says in the movie's defense. "If I had the opportunity to do it again, I would say yes, because it's such an interesting character to get to play. A lot of the time, real-life people can be a hundred times more interesting than any stories writers can create in their heads. And that character was one of the first rebels. He revo-

lutionized poetry at the age of sixteen."—
(This movie is rated R)

THE FOOT SHOOTING PARTY: Touch-
stone Pictures only briefly offered this 1994
short (twenty-two minutes) film for theater
viewing, which makes it all the more special to
those fans who have been able to track it down
on videocassette. Leo plays a singer who re-
ceives his draft notice in the early 1970s. His
fellow band members gather at a party to
shoot him in the foot so he can avoid going off
to the Vietnam War. But they soon discover
that pulling the trigger is not as easy as they
thought.

If you ever get the chance to view *The Foot
Shooting Party,* you may have a little trouble
recognizing Leo. It's hard to believe he's the
one behind the gaudy 1970s bell bottoms and
long blond hair extensions.—*(This film is un-
rated)*

THE QUICK AND THE DEAD: Redemption
is one tough old western town. Herod (played
by Gene Hackman), its undisputed ruler, takes
fifty cents of every dollar in taxes, and in
return he lets the bad guys run the land.

Every year Herod stages a deadly quick-
draw tournament that lures homegrown hope-

fuls from Redemption as well as participants from all over the West. This year's tournament has two unexpected entrants—Kid (played by Leo), who is Herod's own son, and a woman named Ellen (played by Sharon Stone). Throughout the course of the movie, Kid finds himself competing in a lot more than the tournament. He competes for Ellen's affections and for his father's respect.

Although Leo at first resisted playing Kid, he said later that he was glad he had taken on the role. "I had this thing about not doing big commercial movies because most of the mainstream movies are just pieces of garbage that have been done over a thousand times. Then I looked at [*The Quick and the Dead*] and I thought, okay, Sharon Stone is in it and Sam Raimi is a completely innovative director. I could have fun with his movie."

And Leo did have fun. He enjoyed playing a character he considered, "a good version of Billy the Kid. He's cocky and confident until he gets around his father. Then he just begs for attention by trying to prove he can kill faster and better than anyone else in town. He's a sad case but a really interesting character to play."

Besides, Leo got a chance to kiss Sharon Stone.—*(This film is rated PG-13)*

THE BASKETBALL DIARIES: In *The Basketball Diaries,* Leo was able to once again play a real-life person, and make the part totally his own. This time Leo portrays Jim Carroll, a New York poet, author, and musician, who wrote about his descent from high school basketball star to drug abuser.

The Basketball Diaries is not for fans with faint hearts. While the movie starts out with Leonardo looking like high school's hottest hunk, it is heartbreaking to watch him become a strung-out junkie who is forced to bang on his mother's door, begging her for money to buy more drugs.

Contrary to reports in the tabloids, Leo did not take drugs on the set of *The Basketball Diaries.* It's Ovaltine you see laid out on the table. It was obviously the realism of Leo's portrayal that gave reporters the wrong idea. Leo developed the character of Jim not with the help of drugs but with the help of a drug counselor whom he interviewed as part of his research.

"I knew the basics [of what drug use does to your mind and body]," Leo explains, "but I relied on a drug counselor to learn about the specific behavioral nuances."

While *The Basketball Diaries* opened to mixed reviews, Leo was singled out for his fair share of praise. "DiCaprio is a latter-day James Dean," the *New York Times*'s Janet Maslin cheered in a review that must have thrilled Leo, since he is definitely the world's biggest James Dean fan. *Rolling Stone*'s Peter Travers echoed Janet's praise of Leo, calling his performance, "Electrifying! A bust out star performance!"—*(This film is rated R)*

WILLIAM SHAKESPEARE'S ROMEO AND JULIET: Romeo, Romeo, wherefore art thou Romeo? When director Baz Luhrmann went looking for a modern-day Romeo to star in *William Shakespeare's Romeo and Juliet,* he was looking for an actor who was spirited, passionate, and romantic. In short, he was looking for Leo.

"[Leo's] an extraordinary young actor and I thought he'd make a perfect Romeo," Baz explains. "He does seem to symbolize his generation."

Baz made an excellent choice. Even though Leo felt that working on the film was like going to "Shakespeare camp," he managed to make the role of Romeo come to life as no trained Shakespearean actor ever could.

"I've had a lot of teachers tell me that it made their students get into Shakespeare for the first time," Leo boasts with delight. "It wasn't tedious to them anymore, and they wanted to read more."

Teachers and students weren't the only ones pleased with *Romeo and Juliet*. Leo himself loved the movie. "I thought [*Romeo and Juliet*] was good," he told *E! Online*. "Our version seemed to me much more violent and much less romantic. . . . Violence was a big part of that world. It was a whole world of violence. The thing is it's now a world of guns and not swords."

Guns instead of swords is not the only thing that sets *William Shakespeare's Romeo and Juliet* apart from any other film or stage version of Shakespeare's original play. The movie is set in the near future rather than in the 1500s. Instead of Verona, Italy, the characters reside in Verona Beach, Florida. And that famous balcony scene is actually played out in a swimming pool.

The soundtrack to *Romeo and Juliet* reflects this fast-paced MTV approach to Shakespeare. Romeo and Juliet carry on their love affair to the sounds of The Cure, Nirvana, and Garbage.

But the main points of the story still remain. Romeo and Juliet are still involved in a forbidden love. They still risk their lives for one another and their fates are still set before their romance ever begins. Setting the movie in the future and giving it a modern twist only serves to make Shakespeare's words ring more true than ever. No matter where or when you set the story, *Romeo and Juliet* will always be a tale of love and hate.—*(This film is rated PG-13)*

MARVIN'S ROOM: Leo had his work cut out for him when he took on the role of Hank in this 1996 drama. Imagine acting with Meryl Streep and Diane Keaton, two of the most gifted actresses of all time. Still, it's no surprise that Leo held his own in this film, making the character of Meryl Streep's troubled son, Hank, incredibly believable. The film also gave Leo a chance to reunite with Robert De Niro, who plays a doctor, although the two share only one scene together.

Marvin's Room is the story of two sisters, Lee (Meryl Streep) and Bessie (Diane Keaton). Years ago Lee left home in search of romance and adventure and Bessie stayed home to take care of their bedridden father. But now, Bessie has discovered that she has leukemia, and she herself needs to be looked after. Lee takes her two sons, Hank and Charlie, home to meet their family for the very first time. Hank develops an intense relationship with his aunt Bessie, and learns a few lessons from her along the way.—*(This film is rated PG-13)*

DON'S PLUM: What's that? You say you've never heard of this movie? Well, you're not alone. And unless things change radically, the chances aren't all that good that you will ever get to see it in your local theater.

It all started in early 1997, when Leo acted in this small black-and-white film for free as a favor to his then buddy R.D. Robb. The mostly improvisational film tells the story of a night in the life of a bunch of twenty-something-year-old guys and their dates. Leo's character in *Don's Plum* is not a likable one—he comes off as angry and anti-women. But the few people who have seen the film say Leo injected a lot of his charm and humor into the role as well.

By making the film, Leo was hoping to give his pal R.D. a leg up in show biz. He thought he was acting in a short film that after the final edit would last no more than sixty minutes. When Leo saw the final take of the film, it was more than eighty minutes long. As far as Leo was concerned, the long version of *Don's Plum* wasn't up to the standards of the other full-length movies he'd been in.

According to sources close to the people involved, Leo originally had no problem with the short version of the film being released. The sources say that Leo told R.D., "If you have a great film at sixty minutes but not at eighty minutes, let's release it at sixty minutes."

So for now, *Don's Plum* is being held up, waiting for Leo and R.D. to compromise. Until that happens, *Don's Plum* will remain a mystery to the fans who are eagerly awaiting a new Leo performance.—*(This film is not yet rated)*

TITANIC: At a cost of more than two hundred million dollars, *Titanic* is by far the most expensive movie ever made. That alone would make many young actors beg to play the lead role. After all, the film was sure to garner enormous publicity. But it was precisely the largeness of *Titanic*'s budget and the amount of action adventure in the script that almost scared Leo away from the role of Jack Dawson. Big action adventure movies are not really Leo's kind of thing. He's more into studying the relationships between people. Luckily, *Ti-*

tanic had enough of both action and drama to attract Leo's attention.

"I play a fictional American artist who has spent a lot of time in Paris," he told a reporter for the *Irish Times,* "and he meets Kate Winslet's character, an upper-class girl, and falls in love. It's a great story, and Kate's one of the best. There was a lot of intimate stuff between the two characters, and that was fun, but there was so much of the basic work, and that gets kind of tedious after a while. It's the first big studio thing I've done, and it taught me that it's not what I want to go for. But I figured if I was going to work with an action director, James Cameron had to be the one."

Leo was right. James Cameron *was* the one to go with. The writer-director (*Terminator 2, The Abyss, Aliens*) launched the epic motion picture toward box office gold, picking up eight Golden Globe nominations along the way, including ones for best actor (Leo), best actress (Kate Winslet), best director (James Cameron), and best film. Unfortunately, neither Leo or Kate won, but the movie beat out *Amistad* and *Good Will Hunting* to win three awards including the Golden Globe for best picture-dramatic.

Reviews for Leo's performance as the spunky doomed artist were some of his finest.

People magazine called Leo's interaction with co-star Kate Winslet "genuinely affecting," and insisted that although the film has a running time of three hours and fourteen minutes, "it's so involving you won't switch on your Indiglo even once." *Entertainment Weekly*'s top movie critics Owen Gleiberman and Lisa Schwarzbaum both included *Titanic* on their lists of the top ten films of 1997, with Lisa Schwarzbaum saying, "When people talk about the magic of the movies, they mean this."

Titanic certainly was magical. The movie has already earned more than a billion dollars world wide, making it the highest grossing film in history! And *Titanic* swept the 1998 Academy Awards, picking up eleven Oscars, including one for best picture! Leo wasn't there at the awards ceremony that night (he was actually in New York City at the time), but James Cameron made sure to thank his star for bringing the part of Jack Dawson to life. And we're all thankful for that, too!—*(This film is rated PG-13)*

6

LEO ON TAPE

Although all of his films have been quality enterprises (okay, with the exception of *Critters 3*), Leonardo DiCaprio has not had a steady stream of hits at the box office. Maybe it's because some of the themes of his movies didn't strike the right chord with audiences at the time of their release. Or perhaps it's because some of the films were small and thought provoking from independent companies, rather than adventures with huge publicity budgets from big Hollywood studios.

Ironically, almost all of Leo's movies have done well on video. According to Lauren Margulies, vice president of video for Wherehouse Entertainment, a West Coast music and video chain, the high number of rentals for Leo's films has as much to do with Leo as with the movies themselves.

"Often when movies with big stars don't do well at the box office, they do well as video rentals," she explains. "Everyone's heard about them and nobody's seen them, so they rent the movies. *The Quick and the Dead,* for instance, rented really well."

Okay, so that explains why a Sharon Stone movie would do well on video. But it doesn't explain the brisk rental business a film like *The Basketball Diaries* managed to bring in. To answer that one, you have to look at the history of Leonardo's own career.

"Leonardo DiCaprio didn't start out as the big draw for a lot of his movies. There were other people in the films that brought in the audiences. Johnny Depp was a much bigger star than Leonardo DiCaprio when *Gilbert Grape* came out. But [Leonardo] has built a big following that way, because people who came into the theater liked his performances and became fans of his work," Lauren continues. "Now Leonardo is a draw himself, and people will rent films that he has appeared in just to see him. For instance, *The Basketball Diaries* rented well. And of course *Romeo and Juliet* was a smash. Now, with *Titanic* being such a huge hit, more people will want the chance to see his earlier work."

So if you've missed any of Leo's films, you have a second chance. Just rush out to the video store and rent or buy them. But you'd better get there quickly. It sounds as though they're going fast.

7

THE ENVELOPE PLEASE

Leonardo DiCaprio has racked up a pretty amazing amount of honors in his career. But Leo's not conceited about his awards. In fact, he doesn't seem to think that what he does is anything particularly special.

"I can act, and I think I'm pretty good at it," he admits shyly, "but I play pool pretty well, too."

Despite all of his accolades, Leo is still concerned that his success will be considered a fluke. "It's tricky stuff," Leo says of being a successful actor. "I feel as though if you're not perfect in every film, then people say, 'See, he was lucky in just one role.'"

You can relax now, Leo. With a list of honors like the one below, it's easy to see that you are no one-hit wonder. In fact, you're obviously a star that's going to be burning bright for a long, long time.

LEONARDO DICAPRIO'S AWARDS AND NOMINATIONS

Academy Award, best supporting actor nomination for *What's Eating Gilbert Grape*

Golden Globe, best supporting actor-drama nomination for *What's Eating Gilbert Grape*

National Board of Review, best supporting actor award for *What's Eating Gilbert Grape*

Los Angeles Film Critics, new generation award for *This Boy's Life*

Los Angeles Film Critics, new generation award for *What's Eating Gilbert Grape*

New York Film Critics Association and the National Society of Film Critics, runner-up for best supporting actor for *This Boy's Life*

Chicago Film Critics, most promising actor for both *What's Eating Gilbert Grape* and *This Boy's Life*

47th Berlin International Film Festival, silver Berlin bear award for best actor in *William Shakespeare's Romeo and Juliet*

Moscow Film Festival, golden samovar award for *Marvin's Room*

Golden Globe, best actor-drama nomination for *Titanic*

8

LOOKING INTO THE CRYSTAL BALL

What does the future hold for Leonardo DiCaprio? Well, for starters, there's that Golden Globe nomination he received for his role in *Titanic* back in December. And don't forget that the actors who are nominated for Golden Globes are often the same actors who are nominated for the Oscar. The Academy Award nominations were announced in February and the Awards are handed out in late March. Could 1998 be the year Leo finally brings home the gold? Keep your fingers crossed.

Regardless of whose name is inside those little white envelopes, you'll be seeing lots of Leo in 1998. In February, his latest film, *The Man in the Iron Mask,* premiered in Berlin,

Germany. The thrilling adventure, which is based on the classic novel by Alexandre Dumas, made its way to the U.S. at about the same time. Leo has a double role in this film. He plays French king Louis XIV and the mysterious Man in the Iron Mask. Once again, Leo has some top-notch co-stars. Academy Award winner Jeremy Irons and Academy Award nominees John Malkovich and Gerard Depardieu play the Three Musketeers: Aramis, Athos, and Porthos. Judith Godreche gets to play the young girl who catches the king's eye. Judith's character may be unfortunate to get involved with the cruel and arrogant Louis XIV, but you can bet Judith herself was thrilled to get to act opposite Leo.

So, after you've seen *The Man in the Iron Mask* ten or twenty times, how are you going to fill your need for more and more and more Leo? Well, never fear, Leo's working hard to keep his fans happy. Next on the horizon is *Slay the Dreamer,* in which Leo will play a lawyer with questions about the murder of civil rights leader Martin Luther King, Jr. That will be followed by an appearance as a celebrity in an as-yet untitled flick by Woody Allen (Drew Barrymore is going to be in that movie, too, marking the first time Leo and Drew have been on the same set since *Poison*

Ivy). As if that weren't enough, Leo's currently working with director Michael Mann on *The Inside Man,* a true story about a father-and-son conflict concerning police and politics in the 1980s.

In the hot-off-the-presses department, Leo recently signed to play one of the most coveted roles in all of Hollywood. He's going to portray Theodore Hall, perhaps the most influential and least known man of the twentieth century, in the movie *Bombshell*. Hall was a genius teenage biophysicist who was the youngest participant in the development of the atom bomb.

Many young actors wanted to play Hall, but Meryl Streep knew that only one kid could really handle the heavily dramatic role. That was her co-star from *Marvin's Room*. Meryl is friendly with the film's producer, and she suggested Leo for the role. Before anyone knew what was happening, Leo had read the script, loved it, and signed on.

What film Leo will do after *Bombshell* is anybody's guess. Everyone in Hollywood is clamoring for Leo. Leo, of course, is only considering scripts that offer him the chance to stretch his acting abilities. *The Stanford Prison Experiment*—a script based on a real psychological experiment at California's Stanford University, in which students volunteered to be treated as prisoners for two weeks with psychologically disastrous results—is rumored to be in the running as one of Leo's favorites.

Unfortunately, it may be a while before you see these films. Just after *Titanic* was released, Leo decided to take a break from working for a few months. He says he has some "personal issues" to work out, including some minor knee surgery to correct an old basketball injury. Luckily, the Woody Allen film is already in the can, so faithful fans will be able to catch a glimpse of those fabulous blue eyes.

There is one role it appears Leo won't be playing—that of his idol James Dean. For a while there was talk around tinsel town that Leo had been tapped to play the 1950s screen idol who lived fast, died young, and left a beautiful corpse.

"There was talk of that," Leo says of the bio-flick, "but I admire James Dean so much that if the picture was a disaster it would have been such a dishonor to him. Also, playing another actor is a weird thing to do, I think."

Of course, Leo may someday get to direct a film about James Dean. Although he sees himself acting for a long time to come, he says that if he tires of it, "I may get into directing.

I'm interested in staying in the movie business."

Leo's acting technique has definitely prepared him for the directing business. Leo is not the kind of actor that gets completely self-absorbed while he's acting. "I know some actors get wrapped up in themselves and what they are doing, but I'm not like that," he explains. "When I'm acting, I think of myself as the camera. I'm watching myself act. I try to see how what I'm doing looks from the outside."

Leo, take it from your fans. What you're doing looks totally excellent from the outside.

9

THIRTY-FIVE TASTY TRIVIA TIDBITS!

Here are some fascinating fast facts about Leo that no real fan should be without. Some you may already know, but some are secrets that come straight from Leo's soul. Memorize them, and then vow to take Leo's secrets to your grave—even if you have to go down with the ship!

1. Leo's full name is Leonardo Wilhelm DiCaprio.
2. He was born on November 11, 1974.
3. Although he is grateful to his fans, Leo hates being known as a hunk.
4. Leo is six feet tall and weighs just 140 pounds.
5. Leo's a natural blond.

6. His eyes are a beautiful sea-like blue-green.

7. Leo was not James Cameron's first choice for the part of Jack in *Titanic*. (Believe it or not, James says he was looking for someone with more sex appeal! Is there *anyone* out there like that?)

8. Leo attended the Center for Enriched Studies and John Marshall High School.

9. Leo's a big fan of the LA Lakers basketball team.

10. The first place Leo goes when he's on a break during a movie shoot is to the sea. He loves to watch the waves roll in.

11. Leo's pediatrician was Paul Fleiss, the father of the notorious Heidi Fleiss.

12. Leo's favorite bands are the Beatles, Pink Floyd, and Led Zeppelin, but he's also crazy about Wu-Tang and Nas.

13. Leonardo's favorite food is pasta.

14. Leo's favorite drink is lemonade.

15. His favorite color is green. "It's the color of nature, the color of money, and the color of moss," he says.

16. Leo's favorite flicks are the three *Godfather* movies.

17. Leo's favorite actors are Robert De Niro, Al Pacino, and Jack Nicholson.

18. Leo's favorite actress is Meg Ryan.

19. Leo collects five-dollar sunglasses.
20. Leo's favorite song is "Sitting on the Dock of the Bay," by Otis Redding.
21. Leo's first date was with a girl named Cessi. He took her to the movies (of course).
22. *Romeo and Juliet* was filmed in Mexico City. While Leo was there, most of the cast and crew got bad cases of Montezuma's revenge, a stomach ailment that kept the bathrooms crowded. How's that for romantic?
23. Leo has a bearded dragon lizard named Izzy.
24. Leo drives a BMW silver coupe.
25. One of Leo's hobbies is sky diving.
26. Leo has a bad habit of biting his nails.
27. Leo hated his first kiss—he thought it was disgusting. But, being the gentleman he is, Leo has never revealed the name of the girl who gave him that sloppy smooch.
28. Leo loves playing pool. He's a really good player, so don't let him hustle you.
29. Leo's mother was born in Germany. That country is now his favorite vacation spot.
30. Leo wears a thin silver hair band in his hair to hold back his bangs. "It was the most masculine thing I could find," he explains.

Leonardo and
David Arquette
in 1990
Janet Gough /
Celebrity Photo Agency

Growing Pains
with Kirk Cameron
Photofest

What's Eating Gilbert Grape?
Photofest

Nominee
Leonardo
DiCaprio at the
66th Annual
Academy Awards
Steve Granitz / Retna

The *Basketball Diaries* premiere
Vincent Zuffante / Star File

The Quick and the Dead
Photofest

William Shakespeare's Romeo and Juliet
Photofest

Leonardo and
Claire Danes
at the premiere
Mark Shenley /
Camera Press / Retna

Marvin's Room
Photofest

Leonardo and his mother and grandmother at the London opening of *Titanic*
Stewart Mark / Camera Press / Retna

The *Titanic* premiere in Hollywood
Steve Granitz / Retna

Leonardo and Kate Winslet in *Titanic*
Photofest

Photofest

31. Leo's nickname is Noodles.
32. Leo loves diet soda.
33. Leo moved out of his mother's house and into his own home during the summer of 1997.
34. In 1996 Leo won an E! Entertainment Television Golden Hanger Award for male fashion trendsetter of the year.
35. Leo describes himself as shy, but he assures fans that when the time comes to be wild, he can rise to the occasion.

10

WE'VE GOT LEO'S NUMBER

Is seven your lucky number? Well, if it wasn't before, it is now. That's because Leo is a total seven.

We can hear your protests already. Leo's number one, a perfect ten, right? Well, that's all true—except when it comes to numerology.

Numerology dates all the way back to the ancient Babylonians. They believed that certain traits in a person's personality were based on the spelling of his name. According to numerology, there are nine basic personality types. So how does your favorite star (which is Leo, of course) measure up numbers-wise? You'll have to check the chart to find out.

To figure out Leo's number, we first wrote

out all of the letters in his name. (You can only use a full name in numerology. Nicknames will not give a true reading.) Then we matched each letter to the numbers on this chart:

1	2	3	4	5	6	7	8	9
A	B	C	D	E	F	G	H	I
J	K	L	M	N	O	P	Q	R
S	T	U	V	W	X	Y	Z	

LEONARDO WILHELM DICAPRIO

35651946 5938534 49317996

Then we added up all of the numbers and got a total of 124. But we weren't finished yet. We still needed the sum of those numbers (1+2+4=7). And that's how we came up with the number seven.

Leo is a true seven. Sevens are always trend-setters, but that isn't a trait sevens naturally cultivate. They're not trying to be cool, they're just being themselves. Others just naturally follow their lead. That's the difference between setting trends and spotting them. As Leo explains, "I'm not the kind of person who tries to be cool or trendy. I'm definitely more of an individual."

Sevens are also rebellious. They don't accept anything at face value. Leo recognizes this trait in himself. As he told one reporter, "I'm not really the quiet type, although people think I am. I'm a rebel in the sense that I don't think that I'm like everyone else. I try to be an individual."

Sevens work on instinct. Leo uses his natural intuitions to pick out the roles that are good for him. Then he instinctively puts himself right into the character's skin. Remember the way Leo turned himself into Arnie Grape? You really believed he was a mentally challenged boy, didn't you?

As Agnieszka Holland, Leo's director in *Total Eclipse,* explains it, "Leo's like a medium. He opens his body and his mind to receive messages coming from another person's life."

David Rubin, the casting director of *Romeo and Juliet,* agrees. "He has an innate ability to get under the skin of a character," he says. "He's one of the most instinctual young actors around today."

But Leo never completely becomes his characters—that would be just a little *too* weird. He turns off the character as soon as the director yells, "Cut!"

"I would have a nervous breakdown if I had to go through a movie for three months and be that character on and off the set," Leo explains.

Sevens set higher standards for themselves than others set for them. This may explain why Leo rarely watches his own films. It's just no fun for him. He spends the whole time thinking of another way he could have tried that take, and he worries that his performance will not be enough to satisfy his fans.

"No matter how good it is, it's never enough," Leo explains of his performances. "You get the feeling that you've got to give more. It's weird. I think the public expects it."

That may be how Leo feels, but the truth is, it's Leo that expects more from each performance. His fans think he's awesome just the way he is.

So do you know anyone that's just right for Leo? Maybe you are. Sevens get along really well with nines, fours, eights, and other sevens. Does that include you? Do the math and find out. Then find your number on the next few pages and see what numerology says about you.

According to numerology, **ones** are natural born leaders. They are extremely well organized and tend to like to do all of the work themselves. Ones love the spotlight, but they can also get a reputation for being ruthless, so they have to learn to give up the limelight once in a while and share the glory. Ones get along well with twos and sixes.

Twos are quiet and reserved. They are interested in the big picture, and they spend a lot of energy trying to understand both sides of a situation. But twos can also be super sensitive and reluctant to fight back. Criticism makes them brood over hurt feelings. Twos make good matches for sevens, eights, and other twos.

People are just naturally drawn to threes. That works out well, since threes are often leaders. But to be good leaders, threes have to fight their natural desire to want everything done their own way. Threes are a lot of fun to be around, but they have sharp tongues that can sting. Threes get along especially well with fours and fives.

Fours are very loyal friends. They take relationships seriously and will work hard to make them work. That's a great thing, because a four is a wonderful person to be in a relationship with. They are witty and entertaining and always looking for a good time. But watch out if a four disagrees with you. They have a tendency to speak their minds, regardless of the hurt feelings they may cause. Fours get along very well with twos, threes, and eights, but they really go for fives and sixes, who are definitely *not* right for them. Hasn't everyone had a crush on the wrong person at least once?

Fives are like wildfire. They like action, adventure, and plenty of excitement. Communication is the name of the game for a five. She'll never have any trouble getting her thoughts across. Careers in writing, public relations, and the arts are perfect for a five. But she'd better find herself a good accountant—money just slides through the fingers of a five. Fives get along well with threes, sevens, and twos.

A **six** is always kind, even tempered, and eager to help. Sixes always look for the good in people and situations. Unfortunately a six can sometimes be a little too trusting, which makes her an easy mark for people who want to take advantage of her good nature. If you're a six, spend some time hanging out with ones, eights, and nines.

If you are a **seven,** check out the info on Leo at the beginning of this chapter. You and Leo should have a lot in common. Cool!

Eights have incredible powers of concentration. When they focus on a goal, they almost always achieve it. So if you're an eight, go for the gold—it will probably be yours. Eights make great friends because they never forget a kindness. On the other hand, they never forget an injustice either, so watch how you treat an eight. Good matches for eights are twos, fours, sixes, sevens, and nines.

Nines are charitable, kind people, who love the earth, and everything that inhabits it. They are extremely concerned with the needs of those who have less than they. They are the first ones to jump up and volunteer in the name of a cause, and they have little tolerance for those who don't choose to lend a hand. But sometimes that can mean trouble, because the needs of their close friends and family can take a back seat to their concern for humanity's big picture. Fours, sevens, and eights make great matches for nines.

11

TIGER, TIGER, BURNING BRIGHT

In the wild, tigers are unpredictable. They are often tense and ready to pounce. You never know if a tiger will attack or simply lie down and purr.

Leo's a lot like a tiger. When he takes over a part, you never know whether he'll be cold and calculating, angry and violent, charming and romantic, or just plain sweet. Maybe Leo has so much in common with wild tigers because he is a tiger—or at least that's his sign in Chinese astrology.

Unlike Western astrology, Chinese astrology is based on the year you were born. The theory behind the Chinese zodiac is that your birth year can influence how you act and what kind of career you might try in the future. Each birth year in the Chinese zodiac is named for a particular animal. The people born under that sign supposedly take on some of the characteristics of that animal.

Tigers are difficult to resist. Just ask any girl who has seen *William Shakespeare's Romeo and Juliet* twenty or thirty times. They are magnetic characters with a natural air of authority. Like the real animals, human tigers are courageous in the face of danger. Maybe that's why, despite the fact that filming the sinking scenes in *Titanic* sometimes became almost as dangerous as the real thing, Leo never chickened out of swimming through a tough scene.

"I remember how they got one scene ready in about two hours," he told a reporter from *Vanity Fair* magazine. "All of a sudden I'm like towed up on the back of a poop deck with a harness around my waist. There's like two hundred extras cabled on with bungee cords, stuntmen ready to fall off and hit the cushioned girders. And then there's like three cranes around us with huge spotlights. Kate [Winslet] and I looked at each other like, 'How did we get here?'"

And yet through it all, Leo carried on. He truly stuck to his motto: "Pain is temporary, film is forever."

Like most tigers, Leo is almost addicted to

excitement and adventure. Recently he tried his hand at sky diving and almost didn't live to tell about it. Just after he left the plane, he discovered that his parachute wouldn't open. Luckily his instructor managed to pull the cord on his emergency chute, and Leo landed without a scrape. Afterward, Leo said, "I like to do things that scare me. Sky diving is just the sickest thing. I made a little video afterward, where I look into the camera all jittery and go, 'Leonardo, if you're watching this, this is your last time sky diving. It's your first life and-death experience. I want you to learn something from it.'"

Sky diving isn't the only adventurous sport Leo takes part in. Bungee jumping is another of his new pastimes. He also managed to scare the producers (and insurance company) of his new film *The Man in the Iron Mask*, by insisting on racing an all-terrain vehicle during his off hours. A friend he was racing with broke a bone in his leg. Fortunately, Leo came out without a scratch.

Tigers are known as born leaders, and Leo takes his leading-man role seriously, both on and off screen. On the set, it is often Leo who will keep morale high, making the cast and crew crack up, as he did when he moonwalked across the set of *Romeo and Juliet* in a remarkably accurate imitation of Michael Jackson.

According to Claire Danes, Leo's off-screen antics can be really funny—and helpful. "Sometimes I'd be doubled over in pain from laughing so hard," she admits. "That was important, especially when the scenes were intense. It was a real treat working with him."

Leo recognizes that his stardom makes him an idol to millions of fans, and he uses that status to try and help lead them in a positive direction. One of the ways that he uses his new position is to counsel kids about the dangers of drug abuse. After playing heroin addict Jim Carroll in *The Basketball Diaries,* many tabloid reporters intimated that Leo had gone a little too far with method acting and become hooked on drugs himself while researching the role. Gossip columnists gave intense details about Leo's nightlife, claiming that he and his co-star Mark Wahlberg were out all night starting fights in New York City clubs. That of course would be impossible, since Leo often had early-morning calls on the set, which he could never have made if he were out all night partying. Some of the people he and Mark were accused of fighting weren't even in New York at the time.

Although Leo admits that he did not stay

cooped up in his hotel room for the whole shoot, he swears his experiences on the New York club scene were greatly exaggerated. While Leo does smoke cigarettes (a habit he insists he is trying desperately to shake—Leo's no fool), he vehemently denies doing drugs.

"This whole drug thing is very upsetting," Leo told *Flicks* magazine about the rumors of his own drug use. He went on to urge his fans to stay away from drugs. "You see people who have this tremendous need to find a different reality, and drugs seem to be the easiest way to do that. It's certainly not the answer, though; it's a trap. I've seen this with my friends, in my personal life. Even if you have to run away from everything—your friends, or whatever—it's just not the way out."

Leo thinks he knows why tabloid reporters are so eager to tell wild stories about his social life. "People want you to be this crazy, out-of-control brat," he says of the press. "They want you to be miserable, just like them. They don't want heroes."

There has been much talk throughout Leo's career about his stellar performances in movies that just don't make a lot of money. Still, Leo has continued to take on only the roles that interest him. He insists that despite his seven-figure salary for *Titanic,* he's not particularly on the lookout for big roles that will make him rich. He's looking for roles that will challenge his acting chops.

"I want to trust my instincts with everything I choose," he explains. "I want to go with things that have integrity and that I feel I'm doing for me."

It would be easy to say that Leo no longer cares about making money because he now has so much of it. But the truth is that all Leo ever wanted to do was get his parents out of their financially dire straits. Leo has always been more concerned with art than with cash. That kind of cavalier attitude toward money is right in keeping with Leo's tiger traits. Tigers like to work. If you give them a job, they will always give it their all. Tigers are not directly interested in money, they are more interested in challenges. But tigers rarely have to worry about money. It often seems that just as their money begins to disappear, a fresh supply arrives.

Perhaps the best thing about Leo (unless you count that absolutely irresistible smile) is that having money hasn't changed him. In fact, some of his good friends have gone so far as to call him cheap.

"Leo is cheap," insists his pal Ethan Stuplee. "He'll always look for a place to park in the street rather than use the valet parking."

A reporter for *Premiere* magazine agreed, noting that during an interview Leo was wearing "some ugly Shaquille style Reeboks that he got for free just for being himself. DiCaprio loves getting things for free."

Leo admits that he doesn't like to pay for things if he doesn't have to, but you have to cut him some slack. It's only natural that a guy who grew up with very little money might want to take advantage of a few free perks.

But enough about money. Let's talk about something nearer and dearer to Leo's (and his fans') heart—romance. Tigers are well known for their tender side. Anyone who has seen Leo's Romeo reassure Claire Danes's frightened Juliet knows that there's a soft side to Leo that comes through on the screen. You can see the tenderness in his soft blue-green eyes, and quick, shy smile.

But like real tigers, astrological tigers like to prowl around. Leo likes the ladies, and up until now he hasn't stuck with any one girlfriend for very long. Over the years he's been linked to models like Bridget Hall and Kristine Zang, and actresses like Alicia Silverstone and Sara Gilbert. But Leo says those relationships have all been blown way out of proportion by the press. He hasn't really been involved in a serious relationship—yet. Maybe that's because when a tiger does settle down, it's for life.

Leo assures his female fans that he is "looking forward to getting married and having kids someday." But he knows in his heart that "it's not my time to do that right now." Leo also admits that when it comes to marriage, he's not as brave as his big-screen character, Romeo Montague. "I'm probably not going to get married unless I live with someone for ten or twenty years. [Romeo and Juliet] took a chance . . . But I don't have the guts that Romeo did."

Whomever Leo winds up with will have to understand that, like tigers in the wild, Leo needs to spend time on his own. "Anyone I'm with has to give me freedom," Leo explains. "I like to be with someone who has character and style, and someone who is very understanding." Leo goes on to add that looks don't really matter that much to him. "I just like to have sweet people around me," he insists. "Just give me someone who's relaxed and cool to hang out with. I like girls who are intelligent and somewhat funny, with a nice personality."

Whoever ultimately wins Leo's heart will also have to understand his need to be around his male buddies. Boys night out is a regular event with Leo. In fact, Leo is so attached to his crowd of friends that he insists that they be provided with airline tickets so they can visit him on movie locations. Those guys keep Leo grounded. They knew him when he wasn't a huge success and they keep him from going off on any star trip.

"The main thing for me is just to live my life with my family and friends. They treat me like Leo, not Leonardo, Master Thespian. That's all I need to keep my sanity," Leo explains.

Obviously, if you want to be Leo's lady, you'll have to fit in with his crowd, but according to Claire Danes, that's not as easy as it sounds. Leo's posse has a sense of humor all its own. And it's hard to know exactly when they're joking.

"They have this dry, sarcastic sense of humor that they use to test people to see if they're real," she told a reporter for *Vanity Fair*. "At first it was impossible to read them, but finally I learned that whatever they were saying was always the opposite of what they mean."

The woman that does capture Leo's heart will be in for some special romantic private time with Leo, as well. "I'll definitely say that when I'm alone with a girl, I'm doing the baby voices, all that stuff, rubbing noses, the teddy bear thing."

(That's the kind of behavior our dreams are made of, Leo!)

Like many tigers, Leo is not overly concerned with his own physical appearance. In fact, he says, "Being dubbed a hunk kind of annoys me. It gives me a yucky feeling. I feel when I see myself [in magazines] that I'm just part of this meat factory, like 'Wow! Here's the hunk of the month.' That's definitely not what I want to be, and I've tried real hard to get away from the whole situation."

The year 1997 was predicted by Chinese astrologers to be a banner one for tigers. Their businesses and careers were slated for huge growth. In fact, according to one on-line Chinese astrologer, "Tigers should plan and execute and all should come up roses."

That was certainly what happened to Leo. His career success reached a new high when he met up with a character named Rose on board a ship called the *Titanic*. While that ill-fated vessel sank, Leo's career is on the rise.

12

SUPER SCORPIO

"I like to meet people and then imitate the way they talk and walk. I get a kick out of that," Leo once told a reporter. That kind of sense of humor can sometimes sting its victim like the bite of a scorpion. That makes perfect sense, since Leo's birth sign is Scorpio. His November 11 birthday puts him squarely in the middle of the eighth birth sign in the zodiac.

Scorpio is a sign of great power, a legacy Leo is living up to now that his name is synonymous with big box office. But Leo is careful not to abuse that power. While his new status does command million-dollar salaries, Leo is not into asking for difficult clauses in his contract like only green M & Ms or specific

brands of soda, the way lots of big stars do.
(Why do they ask for those things? Because
they can.)

Leo also makes sure to stay away from
power trips while he's working with directors.
Even though he knows it is his name that will
draw in the crowds, he tends to defer to the
director's judgment. Take the time he wanted
Titanic writer-director James Cameron to re-
write the part of Jack to make him more
interesting. James flat out refused Leo's re-
quest.

"Look. I'm not going to make this guy
brooding and neurotic. I'm not going to give
him a tic and a limp and those things you
want," James recalls telling Leo, explaining
that, "Leo's an actor's actor. But great acting
isn't necessarily about great angst. I had to
convince him that it was enough of a challenge."

James patiently explained to Leo that playing a straightforward, non-quirky role like
Jack, was actually more of a hurdle than some
of the characters Leo had played in the past.
He recalls telling him, "That's the easy stuff,
because you have sh— to hide behind. When
you're playing someone who is very clear, you
have to make the scenes work from a place of
purity."

In the end, Leo took James's direction and then sprinkled on a lot of his own natural charm and sex appeal. The combination was electric, and Leo received a Golden Globe nomination for his portrayal of Jack Dawson within one week of *Titanic*'s U.S. release.

Scorpios are heavily into new beginnings, which makes moviemaking the perfect career for Leo. Working in an office means working in the same place with the same people for years, but being an actor allows Leo the chance to work with all sorts of people for limited amounts of time.

When it comes to loyalty, nobody can beat a Scorpio. Leo's loyalty to the people who mean the most to him, his parents and friends, is well known. According to Claire Danes, Leo's devotion and dedication to his closest friends is easy to see, despite that joking comment he once made to a reporter about dumping all of his old friends now that he had hit the big time. (It's amazing how dense reporters can be sometimes. How could anyone *ever* have taken Leo seriously on that one?)

"He is one of the most loyal people I know," Claire says of Leo. "It's one of his most marked characteristics."

Scorpios consider knowledge power, but they find it difficult to learn in traditional environments. Leo is no exception. He admits that he often found the constraints of school life difficult.

"I never truly got the knack of school," he says. "I could never focus on things I didn't want to learn. I used to like take half of the school and do break-dancing skits with my friends in front of them at lunch time."

Leo completed much of his high school career with tutors who worked on the sets of *Growing Pains* and some of his early movies. He doesn't see college in his immediate future. "Life is my college now," he told a reporter from the San Francisco *Examiner*.

Like most Scorpios, Leo enjoys being in control of a situation, especially when it comes to his career. As screenwriter James Toback puts it, "Leo's a very cunning, shrewd, and smart guy. He would run away from anybody and anything that would sabotage him. He does not want to fail."

That's why Leo personally takes part in deciding which roles he's going to play. Although he does depend on his father to weed out the really lousy scripts that are submitted to him ("I trust his judgment completely," he says), it is Leo who has the final say. And sometimes, much to his agent's dismay, that means turning down huge roles, like the part of Robin in *Batman and Robin.*

"I don't care about being a huge star," Leo explains, defending his decisions. "I care about being an actor. I want to take my time with each role. That's how you plan a long career rather than doing it all at once in a big explosion."

Surprise, Leo! By taking such care with your choices, you are achieving both of those goals. And more importantly, you are entering that special realm of actors who have become lasting stars.

13

THE ONE AND ONLY

Although Leo does have an older stepbrother, he was essentially raised as an only child. Some kids might have felt cheated by not having brothers and sisters, but not Leo. "It was great," he says. "I wouldn't have had it any other way."

Scientists believe that the order in which siblings are born greatly affects the kind of people they grow up to be. Oldest children are sometimes overachieving perfectionists. Middle children can be independent and a little competitive. Youngest children are often more relaxed and carefree than their elder siblings.

Only children feel different because they have never had to compete with siblings for their parents' attention. They have no other children around to play with, and scientists think this may be why only children are often extremely comfortable with adults, especially their parents. Nobody in this world is closer to his parents than Leonardo DiCaprio.

"My parents are so a part of my life that they are like my legs or something," Leo declares.

Unlike many young Hollywood actors, Leo has no complaints about his childhood. Although his parents were separated, and they didn't have much money for a large part of his childhood, Leo believes that they did their best for him, and for that he is extremely grateful.

"It wasn't like they created a false good time, that they went out of their way to show me fabulous things. It was just that they were around, and it was great," he declares.

Leo's relationship with his parents impresses all of his friends. As director Randall Wallace told *Vanity Fair* magazine, "Anybody ought to love their parents. But if you look at what it is about them [Leo] most treasures, you get a real window into who he is. And I'm talking about this goodness of heart and honesty."

Leo's parents have always been extremely supportive of his acting career. No matter what, they were there to pick up the pieces when he came up against the inevitable rejections that actors of any age face. Leo recalls being dismissed by an insensitive casting director when he was young. He cried, "Dad, I really want to be an actor, but if this is what it's all about, I don't want to do it." As Leo recalls it, his dad put his arm around him and replied, "Someday, Leonardo, it will happen for you. Remember these words. Just relax."

But relaxing isn't something only children are good at. They tend to keep pushing themselves, hoping that the next task they tackle will be even better than the one before. This can make them achieve high goals, but it can also give them headaches, backaches, and stomach ulcers. That's why Leo tries hard to take time to relax while he's working on his movies.

Many only children are sometimes too dependent on their parents. Leo, who waited until he was twenty-two to move into his own home, is no exception. Even though Leo's apartment is only a short drive from his folks' homes, Leo is often lonely and longs for a home-cooked meal.

"It's a weird adjustment living alone, because you don't realize how much you miss mumsie until she's not there," he admits. But Leo's working on being out on his own. Besides, he has his bearded dragon lizard, Izzy, and his Rottweiler, Rocky, to keep him company, and Leo's parents are still in constant contact with their son. After all, they help Leo manage his career.

Only children are like eldest children in many ways. They often seek approval from people by performing. Being popular is important to only children. Leo had his own special way of getting the kids at school to pay attention to him. "What I would do in order to be popular was put myself on the line, joke around, and be funny. I was always known as a crazy kid."

Sometimes Leo's crazy kid act was a little *too* crazy. His father recalls having to go to school to explain that Leo was only acting when his son decided to spend a day doing an incredibly accurate impersonation of mass murderer Charles Manson. Leo's friends were totally tuned in to the fact that Leo's ranting was all a goof, but some of his teachers needed some convincing—and consoling.

Today, Leo does most of his performing on film, although he is known to imitate people he meets on the street or in clubs. His performances not only have the approval of his parents but of the critics as well. Leo's fans are among the most loyal anywhere.

Only children are often very successful. President Franklin Delano Roosevelt was an only child, as were physicist Albert Einstein and pioneer pilot Charles Lindbergh. Coincidentally, one of the most successful only children of all time was another Leo—Leonardo da Vinci.

14

LEO LINKS

When it comes to linking up with Leo, your best bet is on the net. Leo is a computer whiz, and he uses the web as a way to communicate with his fans. He admits, almost with embarrassment, that, "I like to go on line and see what people are saying about me. I kind of get a kick out of that."

If you want to hear what Leo is saying, you'll need to go on line, too. Recently he published two poems in an on-line 'zine that's dedicated just to him. If you want to take a look into Leo's poetic soul (Leo wrote poetry long before he played Rimbaud in *Total Eclipse*) sneak a peek at *Totally DeCapitated:*

cricketmedia.com/leo/

There you'll find two of Leo's poems. The first, "Untitled," tells of his feelings for awards ceremonies. Here's just a taste:

Nominations and little gold statues and tiny cards.

Nominations, originality, little sparkly dresses, Sean Penn lives in a trailer.

The second of Leo's poems that appears in the 'zine is called "? ? ?," and it begins like this:

Little gestures, little feelings, small strands of hair in your lips. Inside, a world created for pleasure exists.

How's that for romantic?

If you want to bring Leo right into your own room (via the latest Leo poster of course) you'll want to make a stop at the DiCaprio Store:

cricketmedia.com.store

You'll find Leo posters, soundtrack CDs, videos, T-shirts, postcards, and just about anything else you've ever wanted. Best of all, you won't have to click past any other movie stars. The whole store is a one-stop Leo shop.

If it's Leo info you're looking for, there are plenty of web sites to choose from, but Leo has admitted to being slightly upset about some of the lies being spread about him through the web, and now he and his family and friends have set up an official site to set the record straight. The official Leonardo DiCaprio homepage:

www.LeonardoDicaprio.com

is maintained by Leo's good buddy Vladimir Petrov, who is helped along by other members of Leo's crowd of friends, Jesse and Jonah Johnson, Jordan Levine, and Adam Starr. Because the site was created with the help of the DiCaprio family, you will from time to time find information and photos of Leo that you may not see anywhere else. One of the best things about any Leo site is the chance to stare into those sexy blue-green eyes right in the privacy of your own home. (So what if Leo's only on the computer screen? A girl can dream, can't she?) You'll also find paintings by some of Leo's favorite artists on the official web site. Leo feels a responsibility to help his fans develop the same love of art that his parents instilled in him. *Titanic*'s Jack Dawson may be your favorite artist right now, but check out some of Leo's faves. You're sure to become a fan of the fine arts in no time.

Another excellent place to go if you want to be in the know about DiCaprio is the completely unofficial Leonardo DiCaprio homepage:

www.dicaprio.com

This page is updated frequently, so you're never behind on your Leo info.

If you've got plenty of time to spend one day, then be sure to hit the DiCapring headquarters:

www.sky.net/~hack/dicapring.htm

It's the best place to go to find more Leo Links than you could ever hope to click on to. But try to read as many as you can. Every once in a while you may find an e-mail message from Leo. He's been known to answer his fans now and again. Maybe you'll be the lucky recipient of one of Leo's special notes. Good luck!

15

LEO'S LEADING LADIES

Leonardo has been linked with some of the
most beautiful women in Hollywood—Claire
Danes, Juliette Lewis, Kate Winslet, Drew
Barrymore, Meryl Streep, and Sharon Stone.
But relax. Leo's never been in love with any of
them. They're the leading ladies in some of his
most successful movies. Like Leo, these lovely
ladies are brilliant performers with huge fol-
lowings of their own.

On the surface, it may seem that Claire,
Juliette, Kate, Drew, Meryl, and Sharon have
little in common. But they do share something
special—they all have huge respect for Leo.

"He's always very compelling," Meryl
Streep says. "You can't watch anything else
while he's acting." That's pretty high praise

from a woman who has been nominated for ten Oscars and won two of the coveted awards.

"He has a worldly wisdom that he'd probably hate to acknowledge he's acquired," Kate Winslet explains. She adds that Leo is "probably the world's most beautiful looking man, and yet he doesn't think that he's gorgeous."

Claire Danes, however, isn't sure what to make of her on-screen Romeo. "I spent four months with him and couldn't figure out whether he's really transparent or incredibly complex. I think he's the latter, but I don't know."

Sharon Stone says she really respects the way Leo has handled his fame. While on the set of *The Quick and the Dead,* she gave him some advice, which he took to heart. "When you're famous, you've got to accept it as an advantage. It will only make you stronger," she told her young co-star.

Do you want to know more about the ladies who've shared hours on the set with Leonardo DiCaprio? Then read on.

Claire Danes: Sometimes it's hard to remember that Claire Danes is only eighteen years old. After all, she's done so much with her (so-called) life. She starred as Angela Chase in the short-lived (but much loved) TV show *My So-*

Called Life, a role that turned her into the ultimate every teen. (You can catch reruns of *My So-Called Life* on MTV.) She also played opposite Winona Ryder in *Little Women,* and was directed by her idol, Jodie Foster, in *Home for the Holidays.* Of course, there was that movie back in 1996. Maybe you've heard of it. It was called *William Shakespeare's Romeo and Juliet.* That's the movie that turned Claire into a worldwide superstar.

It isn't just the fans who love Claire. Hollywood's elite are tripping over each other in an attempt to praise her. Veteran director Steven Spielberg called Claire "One of the most exciting actresses to debut in the last ten years." Jodie Foster described her as "This wiser-than-her-years seeming person, and yet she's really, really, really a baby. You forget because she's this beautiful demure lady." The usually cynical David Letterman admits to finding Claire "fetching and charming." He even asked her if she could come back to the *Late Show* every single night. *People* magazine put her on their 1997 list of their 50 Most Beautiful People.

It's just possible that Leonardo is Claire's biggest fan. He says he'll never forget her audition for *Romeo and Juliet.* "She was the only one who came up and said her lines directly to me," he says. "It was a little shocking but it impressed me because most of the other girls auditioning looked off into the sky. Claire was right there, in front of my face, saying each line with power."

Today, Claire is busy working with some of the hottest directors in Hollywood. Still, she knows that it is her on-screen chemistry with Leonardo in *Romeo and Juliet* that will go down in history as the turning point in her career. Claire loved working with Leo because they balanced each other. Leonardo made her get silly sometimes and Claire forced him to act more mature at others.

Juliette Lewis: Who could ever forget the scene in *What's Eating Gilbert Grape* when Becky convinces Arnie to go for a swim in the lake? The scene was a turning point for all of the characters in the movie, and it displayed Juliette Lewis's tender side—something moviegoers rarely get to see but always look forward to.

Twenty-four-year-old Juliette comes by her acting talent honestly. Her father, Geoffrey Lewis, is an actor. Her mother, Glenis Batley, is a graphic artist. Juliette comes from a huge family. She has seven siblings and half-siblings from her mother's three marriages and her father's four.

Juliette began her acting career at age twelve in the Showtime network's mini-series *Homefires*. From there she hit the silver screen in a big way, starting with *National Lampoon's Christmas Vacation* with Chevy Chase, and *Crooked Hearts* with Jennifer Jason Leigh. She also made her own Romeo film, called *Romeo Is Bleeding*. If you look really hard, you'll find her playing a strung-out prostitute in *The Basketball Diaries,* too.

Like Leo, Juliette has received both Oscar and Golden Globe nominations. Hers were for her performance in *Cape Fear,* a movie that starred Robert De Niro.

Today, Juliette is busy at work on a new film called *The Audition.*

Kate Winslet: The sinking of the *Titanic* has gone down in history as one of the most horrible sea disasters of all time, but it was almost impossible to feel the pain of the individuals on board that ship until Kate Winslet's performance in the movie *Titanic*. Audiences who watched as Rose DeWitt Bukater fell in love with Jack Dawson, only to see him freeze to death in the icy cold waters of the Atlantic, finally understood what it must have been like for the women who lost their men on the sinking ship.

Kate desperately wanted to play the role of Rose in *Titanic*. She even sent director James Cameron a single rose with a card that read "From your Rose" on it, as she lobbied for the part. When that didn't work, she called the director on the phone and pleaded, "You don't understand. I am Rose. I don't know why you're even seeing anyone else."

Kate's perseverance paid off. She got the role and the chance to work with Leo. That meant a lot to her, since Kate says that she believes, "Leo's a natural. The actor of the century. Nobody can get near him at this point."

Leo was also thrilled to be working with Kate. In fact, he has admitted that having Kate as his leading lady was one of the main reasons he decided to do *Titanic*. Leo is a huge fan of Kate's work.

Kate Winslet has been acting since she was thirteen years old. She started out on the stage in London, playing such roles as Wendy in *Peter Pan*. She later went on to star in several TV series in her native England.

Something happened to Kate when she was about fifteen. She suddenly became very depressed, and her weight ballooned to almost 185 pounds. Her nickname in school was Blubber.

That would have destroyed many girls for life, but not Kate. She struggled to regain her confidence and her figure, and she went on to have an incredible film career that includes an Oscar nomination for her role as Marianne Dashwood in *Sense and Sensibility*.

Like Leo's, Kate's career includes one of Shakespeare's great works. Her performance as Ophelia in Kenneth Branagh's film version of *Hamlet* was a huge success with critics.

Kate's career is on the rise. She received a Golden Globe nomination for her role as Rose and was featured on the cover of *Vanity Fair* as one of a group of actresses with huge careers ahead of them. (Claire Danes was also on the list.) *Los Angeles* magazine named Kate one of the 40 Most Important People Under 40, and *People* magazine declared her one of the 50 Most Beautiful People of 1997.

Drew Barrymore: Imagine being seven years old and the most famous girl in the world. That's what happened to Drew Barrymore. In 1982, she starred in *E.T.* and captured America's heart. That movie was quickly followed by roles in *Firestarter* and *Cat's Eye,* and before she knew what was happening to her, Drew Barrymore had entered the Hollywood fast lane—partying in clubs before she was even a teenager.

"From the time I got famous in *E.T.*, my life got really weird. One day I was a little girl. The next day I was mobbed by people who just wanted to touch me. It was pretty frightening," she told one reporter.

It was also pretty dangerous. By the time she was thirteen, the pressure, drugs, and drinking of Hollywood life had gotten to Drew, and she found herself in a rehab center.

Drew might have lived out the rest of her life as another horror story of childhood film success. But the granddaughter of famed Shakespearean actor John Barrymore was stronger than that. In 1992 she made a huge comeback in *Poison Ivy*. Drew credits *Poison Ivy* as the film that jump-started her second career. Since that movie, she's starred in such high-profile flicks as *Boys on the Side*, with Whoopi Goldberg, *Batman Forever*, with Val Kilmer and Jim Carrey, and *Scream*, with Courteney Cox.

Meryl Streep: Ask Leonardo DiCaprio what he thinks of ten-time Oscar nominee Meryl Streep and he'll tell you straight out that the woman who played his mother in *Marvin's Room* is "unbelievable." He goes on to explain that, "Meryl was such an experience to work with. I've never seen anyone act the way she does. Male or female. She's completely spontaneous. She has such a way-out-there way of doing lines. But it works. And it seems completely real. She's just a master. A true master."

Meryl Streep is one of the most honored actresses of our time. In addition to her remarkable Oscar nomination run, she's won an Emmy for the TV mini-series *Holocaust*. She's also worked with some of the top actors in the field, including Dustin Hoffman in *Kramer vs. Kramer,* Jack Nicholson in *Heartburn* and *Ironweed,* Albert Brooks in *Defending Your Life,* Cher in *Silkwood,* and Clint Eastwood in *Bridges of Madison County.*

Meryl says that working with Leo was a wonderful experience. "He's a genius," she says. But she did have one complaint about him. "He didn't listen to me at all," she remarks, laughing. "And I'm his mother!"

Sharon Stone: Mention Sharon Stone's name in Hollywood and you'll hear people describe her as sexy, or powerful. But Leo has other thoughts about his co-star from *The Quick and* *the Dead.* He calls her generous and kind. Maybe that's because Sharon so wanted Leo for the role of Kid in her producing debut that she paid his salary from her own pocket. "I wanted him bad," she says explaining why she used her own money, "and we'd topped off financially."

Sharon Stone is one of those rare women who have made the move from model to actress with great success. She got her start as a Ford model and made her film debut with a non-speaking role (her character's official name was beautiful woman) in Woody Allen's *Stardust Memories.* But Sharon's big break came when she played Arnold Schwarzenegger's kickboxing wife in *Total Recall.*

Today, Sharon is an actress who is much in demand and extremely well paid. She has her own production company, called Chaos, and she was nominated for an Oscar for her role as Ginger in the 1995 film *Casino.* Sharon didn't win the Oscar, but she did make headlines when she chose to wear a black GAP T-shirt to the festivities instead of a designer gown. By the next week, GAP stores nationwide were sold out of the little black T's. It was just another testament to Sharon Stone's power.

16

THE LEO LOVER'S
ULTIMATE CHALLENGE

How much do you really know about Leonardo DiCaprio? There's only one sure way to find out: take this tough test. Then check your answers on page 92. Don't worry if you can't answer all of the questions. Some of them are so tough, only Leo will know the answers for sure!

1. Leo made his first TV commercial for which toys?
   A. Matchbox cars   B. Hot Wheels cars
   C. Lionel trains
2. True or false: Leo's eyes are brown.
3. What is Leonardo's stepbrother's name?
4. Which of Leonardo's parents reads his

scripts and takes care of arranging his internet interviews?

5. How old was Leonardo when his parents separated?

6. Which *Critters* movie did Leo star in?

7. In which two TV sitcoms did Leo appear?
A. *Growing Pains* B. *The Facts of Life*
C. *Parenthood* D. *Family Ties*

8. What real-life author and recovering heroin addict did Leonardo portray in *The Basketball Diaries*?

9. What was the name of the character Leo played when he was nominated for his role in *What's Eating Gilbert Grape*?

10. Who played the only female gunslinger in town in *The Quick and the Dead*?

11. Was Romeo a Montague or a Capulet?

12. What does DiCaprio mean?

13. What is Leonardo's mother's name?

14. Which of Leonardo's parents is Italian?

15. How old was Leo when he received his first best-supporting-actor Oscar nomination?

16. True or false: Leonardo was born in New York City.

17. What profession does Leonardo's character have in *The Foot Shooting Party*?

18. Who played Leo's mother in *Marvin's Room*—Meryl Streep or Diane Keaton?

19. From which TV show did Leo get fired when he was only five?
20. Which of these sports is not one of Leo's favorites?
    A. Basketball B. Skiing C. Baseball
21. What is Leo's favorite soft drink?
22. True or false: Leo's favorite TV show is *Seinfeld.*
23. What was Leo's character's name in *The Quick and the Dead?*
24. How old was Leo when he started driving?
25. True or false: The first time Leonardo read *Romeo and Juliet* was when he got the script for the movie.
26. True or false: Sharon Stone was so intent on having Leo star in *The Quick and the Dead* that she paid his salary personally.
27. Which of these is Leo's favorite book?
    A. *The Great Gatsby* B. *The Bridges of Madison County* C. *The Old Man and the Sea*
28. Who is Rocky?
29. True or false: Leo is a huge Beatles fan.
30. What is Leo's birth sign?
31. Why did Leo's character want his friends to shoot his foot in the film *The Foot Shooting Party?*
32. True or false: Leo wore fake teeth to play the part of Arnie Grape.

33. True or false: An agent once wanted Leo to change his name to Lenny Williams.
34. True or false: Leo thinks his best quality is his acting ability.
35. With what famous dog did Leo appear on TV?
36. What is Leo's middle name?
37. True or false: Leo is naturally blond.
38. Which two roles will Leo play in *Man in the Iron Mask?*
39. True or false: Leo is six feet tall.
40. In what film did Leo play a poet named Rimbaud?
41. True or false: There's a whole store on the internet dedicated to Leo memorabilia.
42. What did Leo's dad do before he began working on Leo's career?
43. What career did Jack Dawson aspire to in *Titanic?*
44. In what country did *Titanic* make its world debut?
45. On what TV series did Leo play a homeless child?

ANSWERS TO THE LEO LOVER'S ULTIMATE CHALLENGE

1. A
2. False. They are blue-green—and very sexy

3. Adam Starr
4. His dad
5. One
6. *Critters 3*
7. A and C
8. Jim Carroll
9. Arnie Grape
10. Sharon Stone
11. A Montague
12. From Capri
13. Irmelin
14. His father
15. Nineteen
16. False. He was born in Hollywood, California.
17. He's a singer.
18. Meryl Streep
19. *Romper Room*
20. B
21. Lemonade
22. False. Leo loves to tune in to reruns of *The Twilignt Zone.*
23. Kid
24. Sixteen
25. False. He read it in junior high.
26. True
27. C

28. Leo's Rottweiler
29. True
30. Scorpio
31. So he wouldn't have to serve in the Vietnam War
32. True
33. True. Obviously Leo did not take his advice.
34. False. He thinks it is his sense of humor.
35. Lassie, in the *New Adventures of Lassie*
36. Wilhelm
37. True
38. King Louis XIV and his brother Phillipe
39. True
40. *Total Eclipse*
41. True
42. He was a comic-book producer and distributor.
43. An artist
44. Japan, at the Tokyo International Film Festival
45. *Growing Pains*

How Do You Rate?

30–45 correct: Give yourself an Oscar in the best fan of Leonardo DiCaprio category.

17–29 correct: Congratulations! You know so much about Leo, we'll bet you've even seen *Critters 3*.

1–16 correct: Uh oh. You'd better start reading those fan mags. Your score is sinking deeper than the *Titanic*.

ABOUT THE AUTHOR

NANCY KRULIK is a freelance writer who has previously written books on pop stars Taylor Hanson, Isaac Hanson, and New Kids on the Block, as well as biographies of rap stars M.C. Hammer and Vanilla Ice, and teen actors the Lawrence brothers. She's also written for several Nickelodeon television shows. She lives in Manhattan with her husband, two children, a canary, and a guinea pig.

Make sure you have the bestselling
Hanson books with all the info on
Taylor, Isaac, and Zac, each with
eight pages of color photos!

By Jill Matthews

TOTALLY TAYLOR!
By Nancy Krulik

TOTALLY ZAC!
By Matt Netter

TOTALLY IKE!
By Nancy Krulik

What's it like to be a Witch?

Sabrina ★ The Teenage Witch™

"I'm 16, I'm a Witch, and I *still* have to go to school?"

◆◆◆◆◆◆

Based on the hit TV series
Look for a new title every other month.

From Archway Paperbacks
Published by Pocket Books

1345-07

party of five™

Join the party!

Read these new books based on the hit TV series.

#1 Bailey:
On My Own

#2 Julia:
Everything Changes

#3 Bailey:
One Step Too Far

#4 Julia
Nothing Lasts Forever

POCKET BOOKS

Available
From Archway Paperbacks
Published by Pocket Books

1425-03

"Well, we could grind our enemies into powder with a sledgehammer, but gosh, we did that last night." - Xander

BUFFY

THE VAMPIRE

SLAYER™

As long as there have been vampires, there has been the Slayer. One girl in all the world, to find them where they gather and to stop the spread of their evil and the swell of their numbers.

#1 THE HARVEST
A Novelization by Richie Tankersley Cusick
Based on the teleplays by Joss Whedon

#2 HALLOWEEN RAIN
By Christopher Golden and Nancy Holder

#3 COYOTE MOON
By John Vornholt

#4 NIGHT OF THE LIVING RERUN

By Arthur Byron Cover

All new adventures
based on the hit TV series created by Joss Whedon

From Archway Paperbacks
Published by Pocket Books
1399-03